The Jungle Promenade

Xulon Press
2301 Lucien Way #415
Maitland, FL 32751
407.339.4217
www.xulonpress.com

Paperback ISBN-13: 978-1-6628-2236-0
Hard Cover ISBN-13: 978-1-6628-2237-7
eBook ISBN-13: 978-1-6628-2238-4

The Jungle Promenade

A Poem of Childhood

By Ran Whitley

Illustrations by

Alexandra Aiken

On summer nights when moon is bright,

The monkeys dance the tango.

The simians shall
have their fun
And trip the
light fandango.

And yet they come
to have good fun,
The punky and the spunky.

Around the trees
'midst evening breeze
They glide with
graceful dancing.

In moonlight calm
around the palms
They stride while
coolly prancing.

The chimpanzees
with utter glee
Will put their feet to whirling.

Orangutans will join the clan
And set their hips to swirling.

Gorilla girls with hair in curls
Array themselves in splendor.

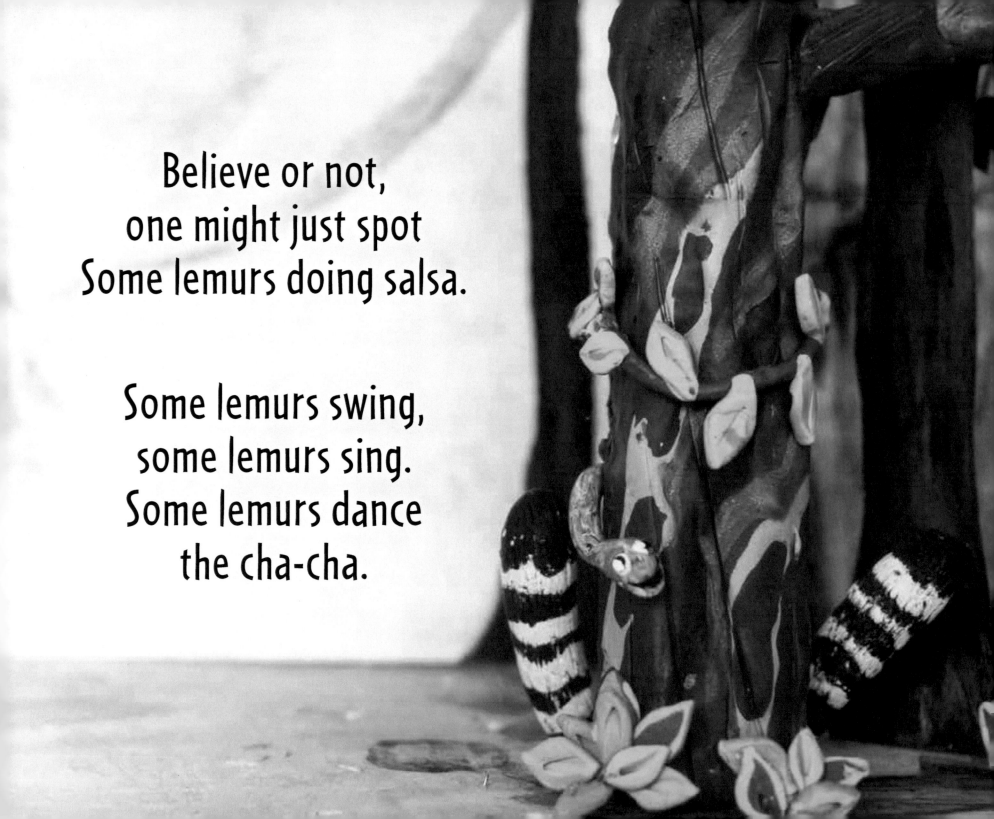

Believe or not,
one might just spot
Some lemurs doing salsa.

Some lemurs swing,
some lemurs sing.
Some lemurs dance
the cha-cha.

The langur spins.
The rhesus grins.

The marmosets are flappers.

The mandrills rock past four o'clock.
The tamarins are tappers.

Baboons with charm waltz arm in arm.
The gibbons boogie woogie.

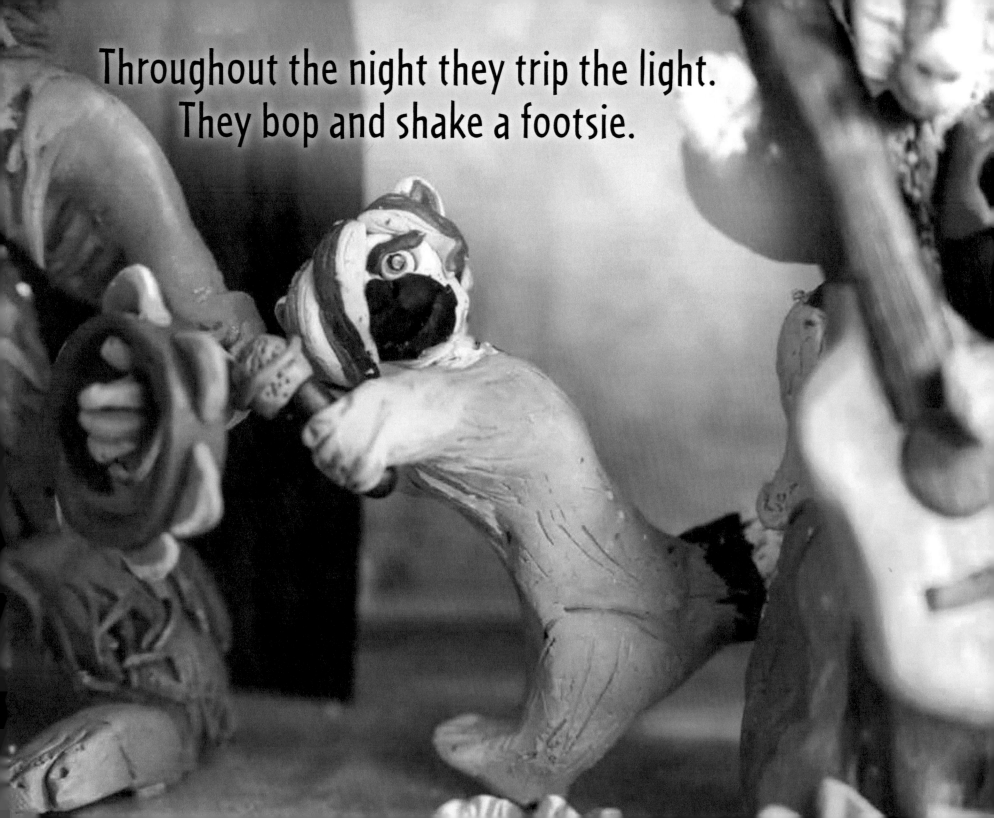

Throughout the night they trip the light.
They bop and shake a footsie.

When comes the dawn the magic's gone.
The melody is fading.

So one by one
they leave
their fun
As morning light
is breaking.

THE JUNGLE PROMENADE

Ran Whitley

THE JUNGLE PROMENADE

THE JUNGLE PROMENADE

Orff Orchestration

Ran Whitley

THE JUNGLE PROMENADE

THE JUNGLE PROMENADE

CPSIA information can be obtained
at www.ICGtesting.com
Printed in the USA
BVRC101811030821
613551BV00004B/22